THE
BARRIO
KINGS

WILLIAM
KOWALSKI

ORCA BOOK PUBLISHERS

Published in Canada and the United States in 2010 by Orca Book Publishers.
orcabook.com

Library and Archives Canada Cataloguing in Publication
Kowalski, William, 1970–
Barrio kings / written by William Kowalski.
(Rapid reads)
Issued in print and electronic formats.
ISBN 9781554692446 (pbk.). | ISBN 9781554692453 (PDF). |
ISBN 9781554694402 (EPUB)
I. Title. II. Series: Rapid reads
PS8571.0985B37 2010   C813'.54   C2009-907248-3

Library of Congress Control Number: 2009942225

Summary: Rosario Gomez struggles to stay out of the gang
life that killed his brother while finishing his high school diploma
and preparing for the birth of his first son. But when his old friend
Juan gets out of jail, his past returns to haunt him.

Orca Book Publishers is committed to reducing the consumption
of nonrenewable resources in the making of our books.
We make every effort to use materials that support a sustainable future.

Orca Book Publishers gratefully acknowledges the support for its publishing
programs provided by the following agencies: the Government of Canada, the
Canada Council for the Arts and the Province of British Columbia through the
BC Arts Council and the Book Publishing Tax Credit.

Design by Teresa Bubela
Cover photography by Dreamstime.com and Teresa Bubela

Printed and bound in Canada.

24 23 22 21 • 6 7 8 9

CHAPTER ONE

My name is Rosario Gomez. I'm twenty-three years old. I stock shelves at the supermarket downtown. I wear a tie to work every day, even though I don't have to. I wear a long-sleeved shirt to cover my tattoos. But I can't hide all of them. There's one on my right hand that says *BK* in small black letters. That one I can't hide. So I try to keep my right hand in my pocket when my boss is around.

My boss is Mr. Enwright. He's a fat, bald white guy who gets mad easy. But he's okay. Some of the other workers here call him Mr. Enwrong. I do not do that. Not to his face, and not behind his back. I need this job too bad. Enwright told me that once I get my GED he will promote me to assistant manager. That would be the most important job anyone in my family has ever had.

I was not always this straight. I came up rough. My neighborhood was on the news almost every night, and the news was never good. It was the kind of *barrio* nice people don't visit. There was nothing there for them. There was nothing there for me either. There was only survival, and I had to fight for that.

I dropped out of school to run with a gang called the Barrio Kings. I did some things I'm not proud of now. Like I said, I had to survive. I used to be the best street fighter around. I didn't like fighting. But I had no choice. I pretended to like it though. I used to smile. That scared people even more. And when you're scared, you lose.

Most fights are won before they start. You win them in your head, before you even throw a single punch.

I was just lucky that I was good at fighting, the way some people are just good at music or art. Sometimes I wonder if I should have been a boxer. But I always used to get this sick feeling in my stomach after I hit someone. It stayed with me. I don't miss that feeling. It's been a long time since I was in a fight. I hope I'm never in another one.

Things are different now. I've had this job for three years. I've stayed out of trouble. I don't go back to the old barrio anymore. I don't even miss it. Now I work from nine to five. After work, three days a week, I take the crosstown bus to the community college. That's where I take my night courses. I'm almost done with them. In just three weeks, I'm going to finish my high-school studies. Then I'll be the first person in my family to have a diploma too.

After class, I take another bus home. I live with my girlfriend, Connie. She's twenty. We've been together for two years. We're going to have a baby in a month. We already know it's a boy. We're going to name him Emilio. We have a crib all set up for him. We have a bunch of toys and clothes too. Connie's Aunt Carlita gave them to us. She has eight kids, so she has a lot of extra stuff.

By the time I get home after class, I'm wiped. But Connie has not been feeling too good lately, so usually I make dinner. I can't believe how big she is. Her feet hurt all the time. So do her hips and knees. I feel bad for her, but there's nothing I can do. And Emilio is almost here. I can't believe I'm going to be a dad.

Mr. Enwright told me that when I get that promotion, I will have to work longer hours, but I'll make more money. I can't wait. I have a plan. I'm going to save up money, and I'm going back to school. College this time. I'll take some business courses. I figure by the time Emilio is five, I can be a manager, and I will make even more money. That would put me on the same level as Mr. Enwright. I think Emilio will be proud to know his dad is a boss.

But I'm not stopping there. I want a business of my own. I don't know what kind yet. All I know is, I can see it in my head. Just like I used to see myself winning street fights. I can see myself in a three-piece suit. I'm not sitting in an office though. Who wants to sit still all day? Not me. I like to move around, talk to people, shake hands, make deals. I see myself in an airplane. I'm speaking different languages with people in other countries. Maybe I'll be selling things. Maybe I'll be setting up deals. Whatever it is, I'll be good at it. And I will make a lot of money.

But right now I need to come back down to earth. Mr. Enwright doesn't like it when people slack off. Not that I ever do. I just don't want to give him a reason to get mad at me. Not when everything is going so well.

Today is Thursday. That means I have class tonight. I hate riding that bus, but I can't afford a car right now. Cars are really expensive. You have your monthly payments, your insurance, your gas and repair costs. All that stuff adds up quick. And every penny I spend on a car means one penny less in the bank.

It doesn't matter about the bus. I don't mind. I do dream about a car though. I know just what kind I want. Not a lowrider, like I'm some kind of punk. I want a serious car. I want a black Lexus suv with a leather interior and tinted windows. I want people to look at that car and wonder who owns it. I want them to admire it. And it will have a nice stereo too. The kind you can hear a mile away.

CHAPTER TWO

It's Friday. I woke up early again. Connie was sore and needed me to rub her back. Man, I'm tired. But I don't complain. And I never slow down. Mr. Enwright never has to yell at me to move faster. Just today, he patted me on the shoulder and told me to keep up the good work. That promotion is waiting for me. All I have to do is earn it.

Five o'clock. My shift's over. I tell Enwright I'm leaving and head out the door. It's a warm day. I like the sun on my face. I wish I had more time to spend outside.

Maybe when Emilio is old enough, I can take him fishing. Or camping. I've never been camping, but I bet it's not that hard. Man, I cannot wait for that little dude to get here.

Suddenly I hear a whistle.

I stop. I know that whistle.

I look around, but I don't see where it's coming from. Maybe my ears are playing tricks on me.

Then I hear it again. This time I see where it's coming from. I can't believe it. Parked on the side of the street is a red El Camino. It's all tricked out, chrome everywhere. It has a stereo you can feel in your chest. And sitting at the wheel is a face I haven't seen in a long time. So long that I forgot all about him.

"Loco!" the face yells.

It's Juan. Who else would be calling me Loco? No one's called me that in a long time.

I walk over to the car.

"Juan? Is that really you?"

Juan turns down the radio.

"No, it's Elvis," he says.

"Man, it's been a long time."

"I know. Get in, bro."

"I gotta get home," I say. "Connie is waiting for me."

"Who's Connie?"

"My girlfriend," I say. "My baby mama."

"You a daddy?"

"Pretty soon."

"Come on, homes," says Juan. "I'll give you a ride."

That sounds pretty good. At least I won't have to ride the bus. So I ignore the funny feeling I'm getting in my stomach and get in.

"Look at you, man," I say. Juan is my age, but he looks a lot older. He lost some weight. A few new tattoos, not very good ones. His eyes are different too.

Colder and harder. I guess prison will do that to a guy.

Juan holds out his hand. He wants me to do the old handshake. At first I can't even remember it. He laughs at me.

"Look at you," he says. "You look like Mr. Clean. What happened to you? Where your colors at?"

"I don't wear the colors anymore," I say.

Juan looks like I just slapped him in the face. But he doesn't say anything. "Still got your wheels, I see," I say.

"My baby was in storage," he says. He runs his hand over the steering wheel. "I only got out yesterday."

"Who else you seen?"

Juan shrugs.

"No one special," he says. "I missed you, man. I didn't get no letters though."

"Ah, you know me and writing," I say. "It takes me forever."

"No phone calls? No visits?"

"I'm sorry, bro. I'm a busy guy. I got a good job. I'm gonna get a promotion. And I'm going back to school."

"Now I know you trippin'," Juan says. "School? What for?"

How do I explain my dreams to someone like Juan? He won't get it. He's been in the pen since he was eighteen. He probably doesn't even know how to write an email or use a cell phone. I could tell him about my business idea, but he'll just think I'm crazy. Suddenly the bad feeling in my stomach gets stronger. I wish I could just get out of the car and walk away. But something won't let me.

"You gonna drive, or are we just gonna sit here?" I say.

Juan starts up the car, and we pull out into traffic. He doesn't even look to see if anyone is coming. So he's still crazy. Great.

"I live up by the Hills now," I say. But when we come to the stoplight, he turns the wrong way.

"Where you going?" I ask.

"I just wanna take a drive," he says. "I ain't been behind the wheel for five years. I missed the road."

"I feel that," I say. I just hope he's not going to make me late. I have to make dinner again.

"So what's up with you?" Juan asks me.

"I just told you. Job, woman, baby, all that. That's what's up."

"I don't mean that."

"Then what?"

"How come you don't wear the colors anymore?"

"Man, don't you get it?" I say.

"No. Spell it out for me."

"I left the gang."

Juan looks at me like I just said I want to date his mother.

"What? You can't just leave the gang," he says.

"Well, I did."

"What for?"

"Man, how can you even ask me that? After everything that happened?"

"Yeah, but the Kings are forever," he says.

"I'm sorry you don't like it. But you were gone a long time. Things are different now."

Juan doesn't talk for a while. He just drives. Finally he says, "Can I ask you a favor?"

"What?"

"I need a place to stay."

I should have known that was coming. Connie won't like it. With her being so close to popping, she gets mad real easy at little things. She's not always like that. It's just hard being pregnant. I will never know what that's like, but I feel for her.

I feel for Juan too. He was my best friend once. He's got no one else. I can't tell him no.

"You can stay, but just for one night," I say. "Now get me home. I'm late."

CHAPTER THREE

Thanks to Juan, I get home half an hour late. That's not too bad. But like I said, Connie is really touchy these days.

We get out of the car. Connie's standing on the stoop, waiting. That is not a good sign. She only waits for me on the stoop when something is wrong.

Connie is the most beautiful woman in the world. She has long black hair and soft light skin. Her belly is as round as a basketball. On good days, her eyes are gentle. But today, they're full of fire.

"Where have you been?" Connie asks.

"Sorry, baby," I say. "I ran into an old friend. This is Juan."

"I was worried about you," she says. "Couldn't you have called?"

"Sorry," I say again. "I didn't mean it. Juan gave me a ride home."

"Wassup, *chica*?" Juan says. "Got a bun in the oven, I see."

"My name isn't chica," Connie says. "Rosie, who is this guy?"

"This is Juan. We grew up together," I say. "He's from the old barrio."

"Oh, great," says Connie. And without another word, she goes in the front door.

I turn to Juan.

"I know you been in prison a while," I say, "but you better watch your mouth."

"Whoa, easy," says Juan. "I was just trying to break the ice."

"You don't need to be breaking the ice. You wanna stay tonight, you just chill out. You feel me?" I say.

"I feel you, man," says Juan. "Relax. I'm cool."

We go upstairs. Connie didn't even leave the door open. I don't have my key, so I have to knock. She opens it after a minute. Then she goes right into our bedroom without saying anything. Man, is she mad.

I show Juan into the living room.

"Wait here," I say. "I'll be out in a minute."

"Good luck, homes," says Juan. He sits down on the couch and puts his feet up on the coffee table.

"Get your feet off there," I say. "I paid good money for that table."

Juan gives me a funny look. But he takes his feet off.

I go into the bedroom.

Connie's lying on the bed, on her side. She's facing away from me. I sit down and rub her back.

"You were supposed to make dinner for us," she says. She always says "us" now when she talks about herself. That's because she eats for two. I feel pretty bad. The baby must be hungry and kicking. Connie might get mad sometimes, but she never complains.

"I will. I just wanted to see how you were doing."

"Who is that guy?"

"I told you. Juan. An old friend."

"I never heard you talk about him before. Why is he here?"

"He's been away for a while," I explain. "He needs somewhere to stay."

"What? No way. Not in this apartment."

"Baby, please. Just one night. He doesn't have anywhere else."

"Why is that our problem?"

"It's not. I'm just being friendly."

"He was in prison, wasn't he?" says Connie. "I can tell by all that ink. He looks dangerous. What did he do?"

"He never did anything. He took a rap for somebody else."

"That's what they all say," Connie says. "Did he kill anybody?"

"No, Juan didn't kill nobody," I say. "Trust me, he's not going to hurt us. I already told him it's just for one night."

"Well, it better be," says Connie. "I don't want him to think this is a free hotel."

"All right, baby, listen. You just stay in bed. I'll make you some chicken and rice. You like that?"

"I just want some toast," Connie says. "I feel sick again."

"Okay. Be right back."

I close the door and go into the kitchen. I take some bread and put it in the toaster. Then I get out the butter. Juan is walking around, checking out our stuff. Our place is really small, but we're proud of it. We have a TV, a stereo, decent furniture. Connie keeps a picture of her mother on the wall, next to a statue of the Virgin Mary. She comes from a religious family. The living room and kitchen are like one room, with a counter between them. You can walk around the whole place in five seconds.

"Yo, man, what's for dinner? I'm starving," Juan says.

"You want some chicken?"

"Hells, yeah. Chicken would be great. You don't know what prison food is like."

And I never will, I think.

When Connie's toast pops, I cut it into triangles and take it in to her.

"Here, take a bite of this," I say.

She crunches her toast. Then she looks at me like she's been thinking.

"That guy, Juan," she says. "There's that one tat on his arm: *BK*."

"Yeah."

"You got the same one on your hand."

"Yeah. That's right."

"So he was in the Kings with you."

"Yeah, we were Kings together."

She chews her toast some more.

"Rosario, I'm gonna tell you this once," she says.

Uh-oh. She only calls me Rosario when she's really mad. Usually she calls me Rosie.

"What's that, baby?"

"You made me a promise. You remember?"

"Yeah, I remember."

"You still gonna keep it?"

"Of course, I'm gonna keep it."

"Because I need you. We got this baby coming. Right now, things are good. But it wouldn't take much to mess things up. You start banging again and everything goes out the window. Your job. This apartment. Me. The baby—"

I put my finger on her lips.

"Don't ever say that again," I say. "You and Emilio are my world. I would never do anything to mess things up. I promise."

"Okay," Connie says.

But I can tell she's not sure.

I'm going to have to prove it.

CHAPTER FOUR

Usually I go to bed by ten o'clock. I like to be up early. But tomorrow is Saturday. I have the day off. So Juan and I sit up late in the living room, talking.

"You got any booze?" he asks.

"I don't drink anymore," I say. "Neither does Connie."

"Man, it's been a long time since I had a beer."

"There's a bar around the corner. But you can't stay here if you drink."

"Naw," says Juan. "I don't want to go to no bar. I want to talk with my homey.

It's good to see you, man."

He's said that about ninety times already. I figure he must have been pretty lonely in the joint.

"What was your time like?" I ask. "You get by okay?"

"It was nothing," says Juan. "I could do five years standing on my head."

"Yeah? I'd go crazy locked up like that."

"Some guys do. Not me. You gotta have what it takes up here." He taps his head.

I can see what he's trying to do. He's trying to make prison sound like it's not so bad. But I know different.

It was just luck that I never went to prison. I was a fast runner. The cops could never catch me.

Sometimes I think about how my life might have been if I did get sent up though. One thing's for sure. I wouldn't have Connie in my life. We never would have met. I might even be dead. I know lots of guys who are.

Actually, I have been to prison but only as a visitor. My mama used to take me to see my dad. That was a long time ago, when I was just a little kid. I barely remember it. My pops was in jail more than he was out of it. He might still be there. I don't even know. I haven't seen him in a long time. Fifteen years, maybe. I don't even know what he did. But I remember him looking a lot like Juan looks now. Tough, lean and mean, with lots of ink.

Come to think of it, pretty much every guy I ever used to hang with had no dad. I think that was the problem. They didn't have anyone to show them right from wrong. That's another part of my promise to Connie. Emilio is not going to grow up without a dad. I'm going to be right there, every day. No way am I going to let him end up in a gang. I'll die before that happens.

"There's a lot of Kings in the joint," Juan goes on. "We got each other's back. Nobody messes with us."

"Yeah? That's probably the best way to make it through."

"Only thing is, they don't let us wear our colors. That hurts. So we gotta find other ways of showing who we are."

The way he keeps talking about colors tells me he's not happy I don't wear mine anymore. Barrio King colors are purple. Most guys wear a purple bandana on their heads. You see a guy on the street with one of those, you know he's a King. But if you wear purple in the wrong neighborhood, you're in trouble. Kings have enemies everywhere. They stick to my old barrio. They never go anywhere else. At least, not alone. Safety in numbers. We always used to say, "Roll big and roll hard."

Juan shakes his head.

"I just can't believe it," he says.

"You can't believe what?"

"How could you leave the Kings? We're your *familia*, bro. You don't leave your family."

"I got a family right here."

"What, you and Connie?"

"Straight up."

"But you took a blood oath, remember?"

"That was before I knew what I was doing. I was young."

"Yeah, I guess so. But it's a crazy world out there. With no family, you got no one to watch your back."

"It's crazy, all right," I agree. "But it's not the only world there is."

"Easy for you to say. Look at you. You live like the man. Big job, nice place, nice stuff. How much you make at that supermarket?"

I tell him. He almost chokes.

"That's it? How do you get by on that?"

"It's not easy," I say. "But we make it."

"Man, I can make more in one night than you make in a whole week. I don't get it."

"No one wants to ice the supermarket guy," I say. "I don't have to watch my back. The cops aren't looking for me. I don't have to worry about prison. It's worth the trade-off."

Juan just sits there, shaking his head. I feel kind of sorry for him. The world must seem like a strange place to him now. When you're in the joint, nothing changes. Time stands still. I know this from hearing guys talk about it. But when you come out, you see that everyone else has been going on with their lives. The outside world keeps turning, but in the pen it stops.

"I gotta get to bed," I say.

"What? It's early."

"Not for me. I'm up at the crack of dawn every day."

"Working for no money, getting up early. Man, you a slave."

I'm no slave, I want to tell him. At least I make my own decisions. It's Juan who is the slave. He just can't see it, that's all.

"You be okay on the couch?" I ask. "We don't have another bed."

"Are you kidding?" He pats the cushions. "This is the lap of luxury. I didn't even have no bed in the joint. Just a concrete slab with a couple of blankets. It's loud too. Dudes make noise all night long. Crying, screaming, shouting. It ain't never quiet in there."

I get Juan a blanket and a pillow and tell him good night. Then I get in bed with Connie. She's asleep. I put my hand on her belly. Sometimes I can feel Emilio jumping around in there like a piece of popcorn. But he's asleep too.

With one finger I trace letters on her belly: *I LOVE YOU*. It's a message to both of them. Little dude can't even read yet. But I like to think he can feel my finger moving and knows his daddy is out here waiting for him.

CHAPTER FIVE

But Connie doesn't really sleep. She tosses and turns all night. This means I don't sleep either. She doesn't complain. But I can tell her back is hurting her. She wants this baby out. We're getting close. Still a few weeks to go though.

I get up early anyway. It's a habit. Man, I'm tired. But that's nothing new. I go out into the living room. I expect to see Juan still sleeping. But he's sitting on the couch, just like I left him.

"What are you doing awake?" I ask him.

"They get us up at six every morning in the joint," he says. "Besides, I'm not used to this much quiet. It feels weird."

I make breakfast for all three of us. Juan eats like a pig. I bring some breakfast to Connie. She takes one bite and locks herself in the bathroom. I can hear her throwing up. I know she's going to be in there a while.

"Come on," I say to Juan. "We better let her alone."

We go outside and sit on the stoop. Juan lights a cigarette. He offers me one too. But I don't take it.

"I quit smoking," I tell him.

He shakes his head.

"Man, it's like you're a priest or something," he says.

"Cigarettes are expensive," I say. "A waste of money."

"Yeah, but a man's gotta live though," Juan says.

I think about telling him a man will live longer if he doesn't smoke. But I would just be wasting my time.

We sit on the steps. It's going to be a nice day. Our street is quiet. But Juan keeps looking up and down the block. He doesn't know this neighborhood. He's alert for trouble, checking to see whose turf this is. It's a habit. I remember feeling that way. Like I always had to watch my back. Old habits die hard.

"You're gonna have to find someplace else to stay tonight," I tell him.

"Yeah, I figured that," he says. "Your lady doesn't seem to like me."

"So, what are you gonna do now that you're out?" I ask. "Get a job?"

Juan doesn't answer me right away. He just sits there, smoking and staring at me. He's making me nervous.

"What?" I ask. "How come you're looking at me like that?"

"Let me ask you something," he says. "Do you ever think about revenge?"

"Revenge on who?"

"You know who I mean."

I was afraid of something like this. Yeah, I know who he means. I don't want to have this talk. But I should have known. Juan can't let it go. It's been a long time. I want to put the past behind me and move on. But Juan is stuck in the old days.

"You mean Lencho," I say.

"Yeah, that's right. Lencho."

"Look, Juanito. I don't want to talk about it."

"I don't see how you can just pretend it never happened," he says. "Tomás was your brother. And he was my best friend."

"I know that," I say. I'm starting to get mad. "I think about him every day. I'll never forget Tomás. But that doesn't mean we need to start a war. You know what will happen then."

"Yeah," says Juan. "I know, all right."

Tomás was my older brother. He took care of me more than our own mama did. He joined the Kings as soon as they would take him. And he was the one who brought me into the gang. He wanted us to have a family again. The Kings protected us when no one else would. They took the place of our mother and father. It was better than nothing. I guess Tomás thought the Kings were the only chance we had to make it. And he might have been right.

But Tomás didn't make it. When he was eighteen, he got killed in a street fight with the Vandals. We used to fight them all the time. Their leader was a guy named Lencho. He was a short bald dude with earrings in both ears. He was mean as a snake. He even had a snake tattooed on his head. His nickname was El Serpente.

Tomás and Lencho went at it one night. The Vandals had beat up one of our guys.

We wanted revenge. Tomás pulled a knife. He wasn't going to kill Lencho. He was just going to teach him a lesson, he said. But Lencho had a gun. Next thing I knew, Tomás was lying in the street. There was a big pool of blood around him. Then the cops came. They got out their sticks and their Tasers, but that was one night I didn't run. I knelt in the street by my brother's body and held him as he died. I don't remember much else of what happened.

It took me a long time to get over Tomás. Maybe I'm still not over him. But one good thing came out of that night. That was when I decided to leave the Kings. I knew I would end up like Tomás sooner or later. It was such a waste. He could have had a good life. And I knew he wouldn't want the same thing to happen to me. I could feel him telling me it was the right thing to do. I know if he could do things over, he would take a different path. I know he would want to live.

"You have to understand," I tell Juan. "I moved on. All that's over now."

"What? The whole time I was in the pen I didn't think about nothing else. I thought you would be ready to hit back. Now you're telling me to forget it? What are you, weak?"

He reaches into his pocket and pulls something out. Then he holds it out to me. I take it and look at it. It's a purple bandana. When I unroll it, I can see a word written on it. It says *MARIPOSA*. That was Tomás's nickname. It means "butterfly." We called him that because he was so light on his feet when he was fighting. It's Tomás's colors. Juan has been saving it all this time.

"Where did you get this?" I ask.

"I took it the night Tomás got…you know. It was with my things in storage. Put it on, bro," Juan says. "And let's do what we gotta do."

But I shake my head and hand it back to him.

"No way," I say. "I promised Connie. And I promised Tomás too. No more banging. Those days are over."

Juan stands up.

"I can't believe this," he says. "You're gonna turn your back on me and the Kings. Just like that."

"I told you, it's not like that. Things are just different now. I don't bang anymore."

Juan sticks Tomás's colors back in his pocket.

"So that's the way it is," he says. "For reals."

"Yeah. For reals," I say.

He stares at me for a minute. I stand up and look him in the eye.

"Your brother would be ashamed of you," he says.

The old me would have gotten mad at that. But I can see that's what Juan wants. He wants to start a fire in my blood. He wants me to get angry. So I just smile.

That's the last thing he was expecting.

"My brother would have wanted me to live," I say.

Juan throws his smoke on the sidewalk. He stomps it out with his foot.

"You think you can make it on your own," he says. "But you can't. Not in this world."

Then he turns around and walks to his car. He fires up the stereo real loud and peels out. But first he flips me the bird.

I don't do anything back. I just watch him go. But something tells me I haven't seen the last of Juan.

CHAPTER SIX

I decide to stick around the apartment all day. I want to be there in case Connie needs me. Plus, Juan made me nervous. I feel like being close to home.

We don't do anything. We just chill. I play *GTA 4* on my Xbox. This is the closest I come to stealing cars these days.

Connie lies on the couch. She doesn't ask where Juan went. I can tell she's just happy he's gone. Maybe she already forgot about him. I hope so. I try to forget about him too.

But the next day, Sunday, I can still hear Juan's word in my ears. I would be lying if I said he didn't get to me. Not because I think I should go back to the Kings. Because of what he said about Tomás. It makes me mad that he thinks I don't care about what happened to my own brother. He doesn't know me at all.

By late Sunday morning, I can't take it anymore. I was not made to sit around the house all day. I need to get some air. And I need to talk to Tomás.

"I'm going out," I tell Connie.

"Where you going?"

"I'm going up to the cemetery. Maybe say a few prayers."

"I thought you were gonna stay home with me."

"Yeah, but babe, I gotta get out. Just for a little while."

"Be careful," she says. "The cemetery is close to your old barrio."

"What are you worried about?"

"You never know who you might run into around there."

"No one will even recognize me. I won't be gone long."

"Stop by Tia Carlita's place before you come home," Connie tells me. "She's got some baby blankets she wants to give us. You can pick them up."

"All right," I say. "See you in a couple of hours." I give her a kiss and leave.

Another bus ride. I sit in the front, with my head pressed against the window. I look out at the city as it rolls by. Man, I hate the bus. An old bum gets on. Even though he sits in the back, I can still smell him. A couple of old ladies sit across from me. A few young punks talk trash to each other. They try to sound tough. I don't even look at them. They remind me of myself a long time ago. In the old days, I would have showed them who was tougher. But now I just keep my mouth shut. I don't need to prove myself to anyone anymore. Only to Connie.

Finally we reach my stop. It looks like it's going to rain. I get off and walk up the hill to the cemetery.

I used to come here all the time. It was really hard for me the first year Tomás was gone. The pain never really goes away. You just learn how to make room for it. But lately, I only come here every few months. I'm too busy. When Emilio is old enough, I'll bring him here and tell him about his Tio Tomás. I've got a lot of good stories to share.

I walk past all kinds of tombstones until I come to the place where Tomás is buried. His stone is simple and flat. It says *TOMAS GOMEZ, 1987–2005*. I sit down in front of it. I'm about to clean some dried grass off his stone when I see something lying nearby.

It's a purple bandana.

I don't even need to look at it to know where it came from. But I pick it up anyway. I unfold it. The word *MARIPOSA* is as plain as day. It's the same bandana Juan tried to give me yesterday. These are Tomás's colors.

So Juan was up here too. I look around, but I don't see anyone.

Oh well. It's a free country. Tomás was Juan's best friend. He can visit him if he wants. I decide to forget about it.

"Bro," I say, "you already know why I'm here. I miss you, man. Not a day goes by when I don't think about you. But I need to know you're okay with my decision. The fighting had to stop. I thought you wouldn't want me to make any more trouble. I could feel you telling me it was time to change my ways. There were a lot of times I wanted to waste Lencho for what he did to you. But I decided to let it go. I just need to know, Tomásito. I did the right thing, didn't I? I hope you're not mad at me. I just didn't think you would want more blood to be spilled."

I don't really believe in ghosts. And I'm not very religious. But just then, a butterfly comes out of nowhere. It's a little white one. It lands right on Tomás's stone. I could swear it's looking at me. I sit still, so I don't scare it. The butterfly wiggles its wings a couple of times. Then it takes off. It flies around my head once, twice, three times. Then it's gone.

"Thanks, bro," I say.

Maybe it's crazy, but I think Tomás sent that butterfly to me so I would know he understands. I feel like I have my answer.

CHAPTER SEVEN

A little while later, I'm knocking on Tia Carlita's door. She lets me in and covers me in kisses.

"Rosito!" she says. "Come in. Are you hungry? I just made some *carnitas* and rice."

I'm not hungry, but I know better than to turn down food from Tia Carlita. She would worry that I was sick. Besides, I love her carnitas. The little pieces of pork just melt in your mouth.

If you look in the dictionary under *mom*, you might see a picture of Carlita. She's a short, round little woman who always has a smile for everyone. She never gets mad. She wants to feed the world. She's nothing like my real mom was. My mom never smiled, and she hardly ever cooked for us.

I haven't seen my mom in a long time. Almost as long as my dad. She just left one day, when Tomás was fourteen and I was twelve. I guess she thought we were old enough to be on our own. Maybe we were. But I still don't know what happened to her. That was when Tomás decided to join the Kings. Carlita is the closest thing I have to a mother these days. She treats me like I'm her own son.

I sit in Carlita's kitchen and eat. Her two youngest kids crawl over my feet and onto my lap. They stick their fingers in my eyes and ears and try to climb up my back. Carlita is asking me questions about Connie. But every time I try to say something, the little ones start yelling. I can hardly hear myself.

"Are all kids this crazy?" I ask.

I must look like I'm having second thoughts about a baby. Carlita just laughs at me.

"This is good practice for you, Rosie," she says. "Soon enough, you'll know what it's like. First one baby comes, then two, then three. Children are a blessing. God is smiling on you."

Finally I stand up to get away from the beating these kids are giving me. Carlita gets a duffel bag from the closet. The bag is big enough to stash a small person in. She unzips it. She shows me it's half-full of baby blankets.

"You can keep these," she says. "I put in some diapers too."

"Thanks, Carlita," I say. "I better get going. Connie is waiting for me."

"You tell my *sobrina* I love her, and she should call me if she needs anything!" Carlita calls after me as I head down the sidewalk.

"And don't forget to call me when she goes into labor! I'll say a prayer!"

As I wait for the bus, I think about how lucky Connie is to have such a great family. And I can't help but think how different things would have been if Tomás and I had the same head start. Family is everything.

And I'm so full of Carlita's good food, I don't even care that it's started to rain.

The bus is taking forever, like always. I'm getting wet.

Then I see something going on down the street. Someone is running around the corner. His legs and arms are pumping like crazy. He looks like he's running for his life. And he's heading right for me.

I don't know this kid, but I know that run. He's scared. Someone must be after him.

I look down at the duffel bag. Then I look up at the kid again. He's just a few feet away now. Thinking fast, I unzip the bag.

"Hey! You!" I shout.

He stops and looks at me, his eyes wild with fear.

"Someone after you?" I ask.

"Yeah," he gasps.

"Get in here," I say, pointing to the bag.

He looks at the bag, then at me. Then he looks behind him. I can tell he doesn't know whether to trust me or not. But I'm not going to ask him twice. It's his life, not mine. I wait for him to make up his mind.

Finally the kid gets in the bag and crouches down. I zip it closed. Then I stand in front of it. I lean against the bus-stop sign, looking casual.

I hear an engine roaring. A red car screeches around the corner and heads up the street. I don't move. The rain is pouring down now. The car slows as it passes by. I look up. It's an El Camino.

It's Juan. And with him are three Barrio Kings. All four have purple bandanas on their heads.

Juan meets my eyes. He looks like he wants to say something, but he just sneers. He's thinks it's funny to leave me out in the rain. He steps on the gas and takes off.

Yeah, well, the joke's on you, Juan, I think.

When he's gone, I unzip the bag and let the kid out. He's still breathing hard, and he's shaking. Only now do I see he's wearing all black. Black is the color of the Vandals. I just saved an enemy of the Kings.

But I don't care. He's young, maybe sixteen. He's got a little mustache, but he's real small for his age. Juan and those other guys would have stomped him bad. A life is a life. No more blood needs to be spilled. I'm glad I helped him.

"You a Vandal?" I ask.

He nods, trying to look tough. I want to laugh. But I don't.

"What's your name?" I ask.

"Martín," he says.

"Well, Martín, I just saved your butt," I say.

The kid doesn't say anything. He just looks at me. Then he looks at the old tattoo on my hand.

"You a King?" he asks.

"I used to be," I say. "I'm out now."

He looks scared, like now I'm going to stomp him. But I just smile.

"What's your name?" Martín asks.

I tell him.

"I heard of you," he says. "They used to call you El Loco."

I'm surprised. But I don't show it. I didn't think too many people would remember me anymore. This kid is a lot younger than me. He was just a baby when I was still banging. How come he knows who I am?

"You know something?" I say. "You ought to quit this life. It's gonna catch up with you. If I hadn't saved you, you know what would have happened, right?"

Martín doesn't answer. He just keeps staring at me. Then he takes off again,

William Kowalski

back the way he came. Back toward Vandal turf.

"You're welcome!" I yell after him.

He still doesn't say anything. He runs so fast that soon he's gone.

Finally the bus shows up. I never thought I would be so glad to see it.

CHAPTER EIGHT

Monday morning. Back to the grind. I show up at work a few minutes early, just like always. My sleeves are buttoned down. My tie is nice and tight. My shoes are shined.

One thing is wrong though. I was so busy taking care of Connie, I forgot to wash my work pants. I'm wearing the same ones I had on yesterday. They're not as clean as they should be, but at least they don't have any stains on them. I hope Mr. Enwright won't notice.

Just then my boss comes up and taps me on the shoulder.

"Rosario," he says. "Good morning."

"Good morning, Mr. Enwright." I stick my right hand in my pocket, fast.

"How's it going?"

"Fine, sir."

"Good. Listen, there's something we need to talk about."

Uh-oh. Maybe he saw my hand. Maybe he found out I used to be a banger. I'm going to get fired. We don't need any trouble around here, he's going to tell me. We don't want criminals in our store. We want nice clean white boys with no tattoos. I should have known better than to think a thug like me could make it in the straight world. Goodbye, dreams.

"Yes, sir," I say.

"So, everything all right at home?" Mr. Enright asks. I wonder where he's going with this.

"Yes, sir, everything's great." Did he see me with Juan last week?

"You still working on that diploma?"

"Yes, sir."

"Good. Glad to hear it. As soon as you get it, that promotion is yours. I wish I could give it to you now. But you have to have a diploma. That's the rules."

"I know. I appreciate it, Mr. Enwright."

"Excellent," he says.

I breathe a big sigh of relief as he walks away. I remember the words of one of my teachers at night school. "Confidence is everything," he said. "The world trusts a man who trusts himself."

Why is it I never got scared in the street, but every time Mr. Enwright talks to me, I get nervous? I got to get over this, I think. I know I have what it takes. It's all inside me. I just have to show it to the world. And I have to be strong for Connie and the baby.

I go into the staff bathroom and look at myself in the mirror. I remind myself who I am.

"You are not some thug. You are Rosario Gomez, successful businessman. You are management material."

Sometimes I feel a little silly, talking to myself like this. But it always makes me feel better.

I tighten my tie one more time. Then I look at my right hand. Some day, I will be able to afford laser treatment. I'll have it zapped off. Then my days with the Kings will really be behind me forever.

Mondays are double coupon days at our store. That means it gets crazy. The place fills up with senior citizens. They take every chance they can to save an extra ten cents on a can of cat food. I know most of these people by sight. A lot of them come shopping almost every day. But it still seems like they don't know where anything is.

And guess who has to show them?

I get paged every ten seconds. Run here, run there, carry that bag, find that product, explain the specials over and over again. And I still have my regular stocking duties. Stuff is flying off the shelves so fast I can barely keep up. Somebody's kid breaks three jars of pickles. Out comes the mop. People walk through pickle juice like they're blind. I hope nobody slips and sues the store. They'd probably take it out of my paycheck.

In the middle of all this craziness, the delivery truck pulls up outside. I groan. It's not supposed to be here until tomorrow.

"Rosario!" Mr. Enwright calls. "Mark called in sick. I need you to unload."

Mark is the guy who's in charge of unloading. I want to say, *You're kidding, right? There's only one of me.*

But what I really say is, "No problem, Mr. Enwright."

Run and get the hand cart. Bring in box after box. Toilet paper, cereal, canned goods. I have to explain to a man in a wheelchair why he can only buy four bags of razors at the sale price. He wants to argue about it. I don't. But I have to be polite. Yes sir, no sir. But rules are rules. I don't make them.

By eleven o'clock I'm already wiped. But I can't slow down. My lunch hour passes. I don't even think about eating. There are so many people in the store I can barely turn around.

Suddenly I feel another hand on my shoulder. I turn around, expecting to see Mr. Enwright again. Maybe he's going to yell at me for being too slow.

But it's not Enwright. It's Juan. He's out of breath, and he's all sweaty. And he looks mad.

My chest goes tight. I clench my fists, ready for trouble.

"What are you doing here?" I ask him. "I thought I told you—"

"Loco, come outside with me," he says.

So he wants to fight. I knew it.

"You want to throw down?" I say. "Fine. But not now. You can meet me—"

"Rosario, shut up," says Juan. "I heard a word from the bird, and the word ain't good."

At first I don't know what he's talking about. But then I remember. He's using our old gang talk. "A word from the bird" means he heard a rumor. And "it ain't good" doesn't need any explaining.

"What up?" I ask him.

"Rosario!" yells Mr. Enwright from the end of the aisle. "This is no time for conversation! Tell your friend you can see him after work."

Juan looks Enwright up and down. I wonder if he's going to mouth off. If he does, what will I do? Maybe I'll have to punch him.

But Juan ignores Enwright and turns back to me.

"I got a call from a bro who was following a Vandal. Something went down at your place," he says. "You need to come right now."

"What do you mean?"

"There's cops all over. I think somebody did a drive-by."

My guts get cold. The world starts to spin.

"Is Connie okay?" I ask.

"I don't know yet. Come on, man," says Juan. "We gotta hurry."

I don't even have to think about it. I take off my apron and throw it down on the floor.

"Let's go," I say.

"Rosario!" yells Mr. Enwright. "Where are you going?"

"Something's happened!" I yell. That's all I have time to say. I'll explain later.

He'll just have to understand. And if I lose my job over this, then that's just the way it was meant to be. Maybe I wasn't meant to be an assistant manager. My family is in trouble. And my family comes before everything. Even my dreams.

We run out of the store and jump into the El Camino. Juan starts it up and hits the gas.

CHAPTER NINE

We don't talk on the ride to my house. Juan drives like a lunatic. For once, I'm glad. It's a miracle we don't get pulled over. But I don't see any cops on the street. I wonder where they all are.

When we get close to my building, I have my answer. It seems like every cop in the city is parked outside my apartment. The street is packed with emergency vehicles. Cops, fire trucks, ambulances. We have to park a block away.

I don't even wait for Juan to turn off the car. I open the door and jump out.

I hit the ground running. I don't stop until I come to the line of cop cars in the street.

There's yellow tape all around the front door. So now my home is a crime scene. I start to duck under it. But a cop grabs me by the shoulders and spins me around.

"Hey, whoa. Where do you think you're going?" he asks.

"That's my place," I say. I point to our first-floor window. Or I should say where the window used to be. It's not there anymore. It looks like it's been shot out. "I gotta get in there."

But the cop shakes his head.

"Can't let you through," he says. "Just be patient. Let us do our job."

"I gotta see my girlfriend," I say. "She's pregnant. She's going to have the baby really soon."

"The pregnant girl is your girlfriend?"

"Yeah, man. Come on. Let me in."

"She's not here," the cop says. "They transported her already."

"Transported her? Where?"

"To City General."

"Did...did she get shot?" Oh, please, God, let Connie be okay, I think.

"Yes, she got shot. But I can't tell you how she's doing," the cop says. "You'll have to talk to the doctors."

"Can you at least tell me if she's alive?"

Another cop comes up. He's a tough-looking older guy with a military haircut.

"You live here?" the older cop asks me.

"Yeah. Is Connie all right? Is she... alive?"

"I don't know."

"Well, can you find out?"

"Hold on," he says.

He talks into his radio. I don't under-stand half of what he says. I stand there for what seems like hours. Finally the radio talks back to him. The cop nods at me.

"She's alive," he says. "But that's all I know. Hey, you got ID?"

At first I think he's talking to me. Then I realize Juan is behind me. He came up so quiet I didn't even notice. That's why we used to call him El Gato. Because he moves like a cat.

"Come on, officer," I say to the cop. "This is no time for a shakedown. This guy is my ride. Let us go."

"Where's Connie at?" Juan asks. "Is she okay?"

"They took her to the hospital," I tell him.

"You look familiar," one of the cops says to Juan.

"Yeah, well, I guess I just got one of those faces," Juan says.

I grab him by the arm to shut him up. Juan has a smart mouth when it comes to cops. He hates them worse than he hates the Vandals.

We start walking away. I wait for the cops to yell at us to come back. But I guess they decide to have mercy this time. They don't say anything. We get back to Juan's car and peel out again.

"Take it easy," I say. "We don't need to have an accident."

"You know who did this, right?" Juan says.

"Man, I don't know anything. All I care about is Connie and the baby."

"Yeah, well, I know who did it," says Juan. "Lencho must have come after you. And he got Connie by mistake."

"Why would Lencho come after me now? After all this time?"

"I dunno," says Juan. "You been talking to anybody? Have any run-ins with the Vandals?"

"Who would I have a run-in with?" I say. "I told you, I left that stuff far behind."

"Well, I saw you up by the cemetery yesterday," he says.

"Did you?"

"Cut the crap. You looked right at me. You notice anything going on up there?"

"Nothing to speak of," I say. I'm not going to tell him about that kid whose life I saved. No way.

Juan punches the steering wheel.

"Lencho must know I'm out. Maybe he thinks we're gearing up for something," he says.

"I don't know why he would think that," I say. "Unless you've been shooting your mouth off about getting revenge."

Juan doesn't say anything to that. But the way he stays quiet makes me suspicious.

"Great," I say. "You get them all stirred up and this is what happens. I'm telling you, if I find out this happened because of you—"

"Chill out, man, I didn't say nothing to nobody," says Juan. "All Lencho needs is to hear my name. That's all. That would be enough to scare him bad. It would send him into war mode. He must have known I was staying with you. I bet he thought I was still there. We gotta hit him. Hard."

I don't want to hear this talk. All I can think about is my woman and the baby she carries inside her. That's all that matters right now.

Finally, after the longest ride of my life, we pull up in front of the hospital. Again, I don't wait for Juan to stop. I open the door while he's still moving. I jump out. I almost break my ankle on the curb, but I don't care.

I run through the emergency entrance faster than I've ever run before.

CHAPTER TEN

The last time I was in a hospital was when Tomás got killed. I hate hospitals. They have that weird smell of medicine and sick people. The smell brings me back to the day when I lost my brother. That was the worst day of my life. Until today, that is.

I don't pray much. But I'm praying now.

Please, God, let Connie be alive. I don't care about my job. Or anything else. I just want my family to be all right.

"Are you Mr. Gomez?"

I turn to see a woman in doctor clothes. She's tall and pretty with red hair.

She's wearing a mask, but it's pulled down around her neck. There's blood on her shirt. I wonder if it's Connie's. I look away.

"Where's Connie?" I ask her.

"We're about to take her into surgery."

"She's alive?"

"Yes. She is alive."

Thank you, God. My big prayer has been answered. Now for the next one.

"Is the baby okay?"

"We don't know yet. Connie was hit by one bullet. Looks like a nine-millimeter. It went in through her lower chest. Then it came out her side."

"How bad is it?" I ask.

"We won't know until we go in," says the doctor. "If we can, we will deliver the baby by caesarian. That's when we make a cut in her womb and bring the baby out. She's close enough to term. It's more dangerous to leave it inside."

"Can I see her?"

"Not now. I'm sorry. You'll have to wait. It could be a while."

"Okay," I say. I know it doesn't make sense to argue. This lady knows her stuff. She went to medical school. I haven't even got my GED yet. "Please, just…do your best."

"Mr. Gomez, I am going to do everything I can to save your wife and baby. I'm a mother too. I have a boy and a girl. I know how hard this is for you. Now, I have to go. I'll come see you again as soon as we know what's going on."

The doctor turns and walks down the hall. She goes through a set of double doors. I look to see if Connie is on the other side, but she's not there. Just a long, empty hallway with a cold, white tile floor.

A nurse shows me to a waiting room. There's a television in the corner. Some stupid soap opera is on. I flick it off. There's a pile of magazines on a table. Who could read at a time like this? Not me.

I sit down and wait.

Time passes so slow, it's like everything is frozen. Every time someone in scrubs walks by, I stand up. I hope it's the doctor with the red hair. But it never is. Finally I just give up. I put my hands in my pockets.

Then I feel something in there. I pull it out. It's Tomás's colors. These were the pants I wore to the cemetery. I forgot I still had his bandana.

I close my eyes.

Tomás, if you can hear me, I say inside my head, *I need your help.*

Suddenly I can feel someone in the room. I open my eyes.

It's Juan. He moves like a cat, so quiet you can't even hear him. I stick Tomás's colors back in my pocket before he notices.

"How is she?" he asks.

"They don't know yet."

"What about the baby?"

"They don't know that either. They're gonna try and bring him out."

Juan starts pacing back and forth. He's all worked up. I've seen him like this before. He always starts pacing when he's mad. And when he's mad, it means something bad is about to happen.

"I been making some calls," he says. "Talking to the boys. They're ready."

"Ready for what?"

"Man, what do you think? To go to war. That's what."

"Juan, I can't even think about this right now."

"We gotta hit 'em, man. Now is the time. They have to know they can't get away with this."

"I'm not going anywhere. Not now. I belong here. Connie needs me."

"Listen, Loco," says Juan. "You may have left the Kings. But the Kings haven't left you. We're still your family."

"I only have one family," I say.

"That's what you think. But this is happening. We're going with or without you."

I can't believe we're talking about this now. Not when I have so much else on my mind. I know what Juan wants. More fighting. More blood. More people getting hurt. More people in the hospital, or even dead. Crying parents. More kids with no dad. I hate the idea of it.

"Just wait," I say.

"Wait for what?" Juan says. "For Lencho to hit again? You don't understand. This is not the way war works. Roll big and roll hard. You don't sit around. You got to do them before they do you."

"I'm not going anywhere," I tell him again. "And I don't want anyone doing anything."

"So now you're the boss?"

"This is my fight," I say. "My family. Connie wouldn't want this."

"Connie is in the hospital with a bullet in her," Juan says. "If we don't hit back, this can happen again. If not to you, then to other Kings. They'll think they can walk all over us. Then what?"

"I don't know. I just don't know."

"Look, man. Real life is not always pretty. Sometimes you gotta do hard things. You gotta stick up for yourself. You think the cops will help you? Forget about it. They don't care. You saw the way they looked at us. To them we're just a couple of *cholos*. And they hate cholos. It's every man for himself. You have to protect what's yours in this life. No one else will do that for you."

I feel tired. All my energy is going out of me. I can't even think straight. It's all too much.

"Just wait," I say. "Just until I know what's going on."

Juan looks at me for a long minute.

"Okay, bro," he says finally. "I'll wait. But not for long."

Just then a nurse comes in.

"Mr. Gomez?" she says.

I jump to my feet.

"Yeah," I say.

"You can come see your wife now. This way."

CHAPTER ELEVEN

I follow the nurse down the hall. We go through the double doors. We stop at a rack with some doctor clothes on it.

"You have to put these on," she says.

"You want me to change right here?"

"They go on over your street clothes."

"Can't I just go in right now?"

"These clothes are sterile. This way, you won't spread germs. You don't want Connie to get an infection, do you?"

So I put on scrubs over my work clothes. Then the nurse hands me a hat and a mask. I put these on too. Finally she gives me some paper booties. These go on over my shoes.

"All right, you're ready," the nurse says. "Follow me."

We go through another set of doors into a room marked *RECOVERY*. There are about four or five doctors and nurses standing around a bed. There are lots of machines everywhere. I want to push these people out of the way. But I stay cool. The nurse waves me closer.

"Connie, Rosario is here," she says.

I step up to the bed. Connie lies there, wearing a hospital gown. She has an IV tube in her arm. There's another tube under her nose. Her eyes are barely open. The covers are pulled up over her stomach and chest, so I can't see how bad she's hurt. But in her arms is a bundle of blankets. And in the blanket is a little, wrinkled face. His eyes are scrunched up tight. He's wearing a little hat. It's him. Emilio. My son is here. He's got my nose.

I stare at him for a long time. He's the most beautiful thing I've ever seen.

I can't help myself. I start crying. My poor Connie. I try to stop, for her sake. But I'm so relieved. It just comes out of me. I've never cried in front of Connie before. I was brought up to believe that men don't cry. I'm just glad she's asleep. And I'm glad the baby doesn't know what's going on. I don't want his first memory of his daddy to be this. What a way to start out your life.

"I know you're upset, but try to stay calm," says the doctor. "We don't want to upset her."

Sometimes keeping cool is the hardest thing in the world. But I pull myself together. Then I bend down and kiss Connie. Her eyes flutter open.

"Rosie?" she whispers. "Is that you?"

"It's better if she doesn't talk," says the red-haired doctor. "She needs to rest. You can only stay a minute."

"Connie," I say. "Don't try to talk. Just listen. The baby is out. He's perfect. And you're going to be okay."

I can tell Connie is trying to smile. But she's too weak. I'm trying to hold it together. What I want to do is break every window in the place. I think about how much pain she must be in, and I get angry. More angry than when I lost Tomás. But now is not the time to lose it. I have to forget about my own feelings. I need to think about my family instead.

I turn to the red-haired doctor.

"Is the baby okay?" I ask.

"The baby is fine. The bullet missed him. It bounced off Connie's rib and went out again, without doing major damage to her organs. She was very lucky. She's going to have to take it easy for a long time though."

Thank you, God, I think. And thank you, Tomás.

"Let's leave the Gomezes alone for a minute," the red-haired doctor announces to everyone. "But only a minute, Mr. Gomez. Your wife really needs to rest."

Everyone steps out of the room.

"Rosie," Connie whispers. "Why?"

I know what she means. She wants to know why this happened. And I want to tell her, *Because I didn't do what I should have done a long time ago.* But I can't say that. Not now.

"It was a mistake," I say instead. "Shh. It's all over now. You're safe. I'm gonna take care of you."

"But…you promised. No more banging."

"I didn't break my promise, honey."

"You…swear?"

"I swear. I love you, baby."

"Love…you…too."

Connie closes her eyes. I can hear the doctors coming back in the room. But I want just one more minute with my son. I wish I could pick him up. But he looks so tiny, I might break him. So I just reach out and touch his nose. He wrinkles his face and makes a sound like a kitten. Connie seems to hear him. She moans.

"Listen, little dude," I whisper. "I'm your papa. And I'm gonna give you all the things I never had. You're gonna have a great life. You'll have a mama and a papa who love you. You'll have a nice safe house. You'll get an education. I'm going to give you all these things, no matter what. That's my promise to you."

I wonder if he knows my voice. I talked to him all the time when he was inside. They say babies can hear you even before they're born.

"Can I just stay with her?" I ask the red-haired doctor. "I won't talk."

But she shakes her head.

"I understand your feelings," she says. "But she won't get better if she doesn't rest. She got shot and delivered a baby in the same day. She's very weak. We have to keep a close eye on her. You should go home and come back in the morning."

Morning? I don't even know what time it is. How long have I been here? I look at the clock. It says nine. Somehow I lost the whole day. That's okay. I'd rather lose one day of my life than lose my wife and son. Who am I kidding? I'd give up every day I have left if I knew it would make them safe.

I turn and head for the door. But I stop and look back at the doctor.

"Thank you for everything," I say to her. "I'll never forget you."

"You're welcome, Rosario," she says.

I go out the double doors. I take off my scrubs. A nurse shows me where to put them.

But before I go back into the waiting room, I stop and think.

Juan is right. I don't want war, but we can't just do nothing. Those Vandals won't stop until they get me and Juan both.

And he's right about life not being pretty. Sometimes a man has to do hard things if he wants to survive. That was a lesson I learned a long time ago. I was stupid to think that things are any different now.

There is another choice. I can wait for Connie to get better, and then we can leave this city and never come back.

But my whole life is here. My job. My school. Connie's family. No way can we leave.

So, I have to fight. War is defending what you love. And I love Connie and Emilio so much there is nothing I won't do to keep them safe.

I reach into my pocket and pull out Tomás's colors. I look at his name, *MARIPOSA*. I think back to the cemetery, when that butterfly came like a message from my brother.

"Tomás," I whisper, "I asked you if I did the right thing before, and you sent me a sign. But things are different now. So I'm asking you again for help. Show me the way, brother. Let me know what to do."

I wait. But nothing happens.

Then I feel kind of stupid. What did I expect? Another butterfly here in the hospital?

Never mind, I think. Sometimes you have to find your own answers.

And I know what I need to do.

I put Tomás's colors on. I tighten the bandana around my head. Then I go into the waiting room.

Juan is still there. He's pacing back and forth. He looks up at me. Then he looks at the colors on my head. He doesn't say anything. He just nods. Then he holds out his hand. We do the old handshake. I remember it now. It comes back to me like I just did it yesterday.

We leave the hospital together, without saying a word.

CHAPTER TWELVE

There are four of us in the car. Juan is driving. I sit next to him. In the back are two Kings I've never met before. They're a few years younger than me. They must have got jumped in after I left. Both of them are covered in tattoos. One is named Chucho. He's one of the ugliest dudes I've ever seen, with buckteeth and a broken nose. But he's got a killer's eyes.

The other one is named Snap. He's tall and thin, with a scar on his neck where someone must have slashed him. Both of them are hard as steel. The kind of guys I didn't want to be around anymore. But

I'm glad they're here now. Now that it's time for action.

I've been up all night. But I'm not tired. I can feel my blood pumping through my body. I feel ready for anything. Ready to die, even.

There are just a few cars on the road. The city is still asleep. The sky is dark. The sun will be up in an hour. Everything looks so peaceful. It's hard to imagine there's anything wrong in the world.

We roll quiet. No music. No one says a word. Everyone is thinking about what's coming. I remember that movie about D-Day, *Saving Private Ryan*. All those guys in the boats, heading for the beach. Waiting to attack. Waiting to die. Some of them were so scared they were puking. When I saw that movie, I knew just how they felt. I felt that way plenty of times before. I never thought I would feel that way again. But I'm feeling it now.

No way am I going to get sick though. Not in front of these guys. They would just see it as a sign of weakness. And I don't feel weak. I feel strong. Ready to do what I have to do.

We head into Vandal territory.

To regular people, the world of the Vandals looks no different than the world of the Barrio Kings. Same buildings, same sidewalks, same stoops, same everything. But when you're a King, being on Vandal turf feels like being on the moon. Even the air tastes different. You feel different too. I can feel the guys in the car get tense. Everyone is on the lookout for something. Anything. Our nerves are electric. You could light up the whole city with the energy in the car right now.

We pull up to the curb. Juan kills the engine. No one makes a sound. A block away, I can see a little house on the corner. Lencho's house. The windows are dark. We sit and watch for a minute. Nothing happens. My heart is pounding so loud, I'm surprised it doesn't wake up the neighbors.

"You ready?" Juan says to me.

Back at Chucho's place, we came up with a plan together. And I came up with a plan of my own. Now it's time to put it into action. Not his. Mine. Juan doesn't know that yet. But he will soon enough.

"Yeah, *ese*, I'm ready," I say.

Juan opens the glove compartment and pulls out a gun. It's a .45, a big honking pistol. It's been a while since I handled a gun. But it's just like riding a bike. Once you learn, you never forget.

I pop the clip and check it. It's full of rounds. Then I slide it back in. The noise it makes is solid, serious. There's no other sound like that in the world.

"Put one in the chamber," says Juan.

But I shake my head. I let him think I was going along with what he wanted. But I have an idea of how to handle this. I convinced the three of them to let me go in first, alone. They didn't fight me on it. I may have been out of the gang awhile, but my rep is still strong. They know I can handle anything.

I stick the gun in my waistband, in the small of my back. That was always my favorite place to carry. Lots of bangers wear saggy pants, but I never did. It never made sense to me. When you sag, you can't run. And you have nowhere to hide a piece.

"Five minutes, like we said," I say. "Then you guys come in."

Juan nods. I look back at Chucho and Snap.

"You with me?" I say.

They just nod. No words. Good. I hate it when guys talk too much. These guys are made of iron. They're soldiers, the best of the best. They're Kings.

I open the door and slide out. Then I push it closed, careful not to make a sound. I'm wearing a T-shirt with no sleeves. I can feel the cool air on my shoulders. For the first time in five years, my tats are there for the world to see. I'm doing something I said I would never do again. I'm representing the Kings.

I walk down the street, fast, moving like a ghost. I look all around, but I don't see anyone. I hop the fence and land in the front yard. Then I run in a crouch to the back corner. No dogs. Good. I like dogs. I would hate to have to shoot one.

I look at my watch. Four minutes left. I force myself to wait another minute. Then I stick my head around the corner.

There's the back door, just like Juan said. There's a little porch. I can see someone sitting on it. Juan told me about him too. Lencho always leaves a guard at the back door. The front door would be too obvious. This Vandal is in a chair, and his back is to me. I pull the .45 from my pants and come up behind him.

The guard is half asleep, resting his head on his arms. But he feels me come up behind him. He starts to get up.

Sorry, dude, I think.

I bring the handle of the .45 down on his head, hard. He goes down like a bag of wet laundry. He lands on his back. I don't want to look at his face, but I can't help it.

It's Martín. That kid I saved from the bus stop.

I feel bad for a second. But there's no time to think about it. I gotta do this. I check Martín's pants. There's a piece in his pocket. I take it and stick it in my waistband. Now I have two guns.

Just try and stop me, I think.

The back door has a little window in it. I look in. I don't see anyone. I wiggle the knob. It's locked, but I know how to deal with that. Out comes my driver's license. I stick it in between the door and the frame. The door opens nice and quiet. I slide inside. I pull Martín in after me and close the door.

The house is dark. I'm in the kitchen. It's a mess. Beer cans everywhere. No food in sight. It reminds me of our kitchen when Tomás and I were growing up.

Ahead of me is the living room. It's got a couch in it and not much else. No one there. Good. I don't need to fight a whole army.

I check my watch again. Three minutes left. I stand still and force myself to wait another minute. Time never passed more slowly. But I need to listen. And I need to calm down. The blood is raging in my ears. But soon it quiets down.

Then, I can hear someone snoring.

I see a hallway. That must be where the bedrooms are. I walk real slow. I've got my .45 out in front of me, like I'm a cop on television. I flick the safety off. But I keep my finger off the trigger. I don't want the gun to fire by mistake. All those stories you read in the paper about innocent people getting killed flash through my mind. Bullets can fly a long way. Most idiots don't know anything about guns. Not me. I've got lots of practice.

There are two bedroom doors. One is open, the other is half-closed. I look in the open one. There's a bed, but it's empty.

I turn and move toward the half-closed door. The snoring gets louder.

I check my watch again. One minute left. Time to do it.

I kick open the door, pointing the gun in front of me.

"Get up!" I scream. "Get up! Get up now!"

Then I stop. I wasn't ready for this.

Lencho is there, lying in bed in his underwear. I was ready for him.

Lying next to him is a woman. She's in a nightgown. I was ready for her too.

But between them lies a little baby in a diaper, no more than a year old.

And that is what I wasn't ready for.

Damn you, Juan, I think. Why didn't you tell me Lencho had a kid?

CHAPTER THIRTEEN

The woman wakes up first. She sits up and starts screaming.

"Lencho!" she shrieks.

Lencho is up like a shot. He stares around, wild-eyed. When he sees me, he makes a move under his pillow. But I aim the gun at his head and step forward fast.

"Don't do it," I say. "Hands on your head. You too, lady."

They do as they're told. Lencho is looking at me in shock. Then his eyes get narrow, like a snake's. I've seen that look on him before. It's the same look he had the night he shot my brother.

The baby wakes up. I can tell by her earrings it's a little girl. She starts to cry.

"You move, I shoot," I say.

"Let me pick up my baby!" screams Lencho's woman.

Lencho is still looking at me with those snake eyes. I stare him down.

"You wanna make a move?" I ask him. "Go ahead, if you're feeling brave."

Slowly, he shakes his head no.

"Go ahead and pick up the baby," I say to his woman. "But do it slow. And then get out of the way."

The woman takes the baby girl in her arms. She slides off the bed onto the floor. She and the baby are both crying. If Lencho could kill me with his eyes, I would have been dead five seconds ago.

I move forward and press my gun against his head. Then I reach under his pillow.

I take out the gun he was about to grab. It's a 9-millimeter. The same kind of gun that Connie got shot with.

"Any more guns in here?" I ask.

He shakes his head.

"You know what this is about?" I say.

"No," he says. "Who are you?"

"You mean you don't recognize me?"

He looks harder at my face. Then he looks at the ink on my shoulders. My gang name is written there, in big letters. His eyes get wide.

"Loco," he says.

"That's right."

"So this is about Tomás."

"No, it's not about Tomás!" I yell. "It's about Connie! My girlfriend! The one you shot yesterday!"

Just then I hear the back door get kicked in. There's more yelling. Juan, Chucho and Snap are right on time.

"Back here!" I yell.

The three of them come tumbling in the door. Their guns are out. I hold my hand up.

"There's no one else here," I say to them. "Except that punk I laid out. I got this. You guys chill."

"Do it, man," says Juan. "What are you waiting for?"

"Smoke him, homes," says Chucho. "Follow the plan."

"Wait a minute. I don't know nothing about no Connie," says Lencho.

"Save your lies," I tell him.

"It's true. I swear. And about Tomás. You know I had to do it. It was him or me."

"You shoulda known the Kings would come for you one day," says Juan. He raises his gun and points it at Lencho. His girlfriend starts screaming again. The baby cries louder.

"Loco, this is your gig, but if you don't do it, I will," Juan says to me.

"Wait a minute," I say. "Lencho. You didn't shoot Connie?"

Lencho stares at me. He shakes his head.

"You gonna waste me for your brother, fine," he says. "Maybe I got it coming. But you gotta know I didn't do nobody named Connie. I ain't done anything."

I keep looking at the girl holding her baby. They're both looking back at me, terrified. Suddenly I see myself through their eyes. And I hate what I see. I'm the monster in the night, come to destroy everything they love. I'm the nightmare this baby will have the rest of her life.

Besides, I wasn't going to kill Lencho. That was Juan's plan, not mine. And something makes me think Lencho is telling the truth.

"Somebody did a drive-by at my place," I tell him. "No way it was a mistake. Someone was after me. Who was it?"

"I don't know, man, I'm telling you."

"He's lying!" Juan shouts.

"No," I say. "I don't think so."

"Man, are you whack?" Snap says. "I can't believe this. Of course he's lying."

"You guys got some *cojones*, coming into my place like this," says Lencho. "You wanna start a war? The Vandals will burn the city down to get you."

"The war already got started," Juan says.

"Not by me," says Lencho.

"Loco, this is your last chance to make it right," says Juan. "I got a big old cap to bust. And I wanna put in the work bad."

Suddenly I don't know what to do. I can't think with that baby crying. The room is hot, like a sauna. My head is spinning. All I can think about is Connie and Emilio.

And then I think about Tomás. He sent me a sign, all right. And back in the hospital, when I asked him to show me another one, he answered me. Only I was too stupid to see it. What he showed me was nothing. Because that is what the future will be, if I keep going down this path.

You know that old saying, *He who hesitates is lost*? I heard my teacher at the community college say that. What he meant was, if you think but don't act, you don't know what's gonna happen.

Well, I hesitated, all right. Just a second too long.

"Everybody down!" someone yells from the door.

I turn to see who it is.

Man, I should have hit that kid harder. Because here is Martín in the doorway, with blood dripping down his forehead, and a gun in his arms. Not a pistol. A rifle. Looks like an AK. Got a big banana clip sticking out the top. And it's pointed right at me.

"Everybody down!" he yells again. "Lencho, tell me what to do!"

I look back at Lencho. I lower my gun. His eyes get narrow again.

I hesitated. And now I'm lost.

We all are.

CHAPTER FOURTEEN

I don't move. But Martín yells again.

"Drop your gats!" he says.

I put down my .45. Juan, Chucho and Snap drop their guns. I still have Martín's piece in my waistband. For a minute, I think I'll get away with that. But he's still pointing the gun at me.

He says, "Gimme my piece back."

"What piece?" I say.

"Man, do not mess with me! I know you got my nine."

"You little punk. I shoulda wasted you when I had the chance," Juan snarls.

Martín points his AK at Juan and racks a round. I swear, he's about to pull the trigger. Juan doesn't even flinch. I have to say one thing about Juan. He's afraid of nothing. Not even getting shot in the face.

"I'll get to you in a minute," says Martín.

He's sweating, and his voice is high. The kid is scared. That worries me. Scared people can do anything.

Then the gun swings around again. It's pointed at me once more.

"And what are you doing here? I thought I wasted you yesterday," he says.

For a minute, there's not a sound.

"You," I say finally. "You shot Connie? After what I did for you? You tried to kill me?"

"Oh, man. I am gonna slice you open," says Snap to Martín.

Around the AK swings again, this time to point at Snap. Martín aims carefully. He's about to pull the trigger.

But Lencho says, "No."

The kid looks at him.

"What did you say?" he says.

"You heard me," says Lencho.

Martín looks like he just got spanked by his daddy. All the air goes out of the room.

"Who told you to do anything?" Lencho says to Martín.

"Nobody. I just—"

"You just what?" snarls Juan. "You thought you could be a man. Is that it?"

"This little punk was trying to make his bones," says Chucho. "So he could be a senior member. A big man."

"Is that right?" says Lencho.

Martín looks even more scared of Lencho than he is of us. He nods.

"You know the rules," Lencho says. "Nobody makes a move without orders."

We all stand there, waiting. I have no idea what is going to happen next. So I decide to say something.

"Lencho, listen up," I say. "I didn't come here to kill you."

"No?" says Lencho. "You just dropped by for a cup of tea?"

"I had to get your attention. And I didn't know the baby was here. Listen, man. I came here to tell you this has to end. I left the Kings five years ago."

"I know you did," says Lencho. "So imagine my surprise to see you in my own crib, pointing a gat at my head."

"Like I said, I didn't come here to kill you. I just wanted to talk."

"I can't believe this crap," says Snap. "What do you mean, you didn't come here to kill him?"

"I had my own plan," I say. "I just needed you guys to get me inside and back me up."

"You played us," says Chucho.

"I didn't mean to play anyone. I don't want anyone getting killed. I just want to talk."

"So talk," says Lencho.

"This little punk," I say, pointing to Martín, "was running for his life the other day on the street. And I saved him from getting stomped. I hid him in my bag."

"You did *what*?" says Juan. "You lied to me?"

"I did it because I don't want no more of this," I say. "This is all craziness. What you said about why you shot Tomás, Lencho. I know you had no choice. That was what I came here to tell you. Even though I thought it was you who shot Connie, I wasn't gonna kill you. I figured you did it because you were scared. I was mad, all right. But I was gonna tell you things need to stop here. But now I know who did it. It was him. And that makes everything different."

"So you wanted to be a big man," Lencho says to Martín.

He gets up off the bed and steps toward the kid.

"Put that thing down," he says. "Who told you you could touch my AK anyway? That's for big boys only."

"But...I...," Martín stammers.

"Do it," says Lencho.

Martín doesn't dare not listen. Lencho is his master. He puts the gun down.

And then Lencho lashes out. His fist flies into the kid's face. Martín goes down with a scream. Lencho gets on top of him. He starts punching him in the face, hard. And with every punch, he talks to him, in a calm voice. It's weird how quiet his voice is.

"You don't know how bad you messed things up."

Smack.

"You almost brought everything down."

Thud.

"You never do something like that without orders."

Whack.

Martín is a bloody, crying mess by the time Lencho is done. Lencho stands up, breathing hard.

"You," he says to me. "Loco."

"Yeah."

"What you said about not coming here to shoot me. Was that true?"

"Yeah, man, it was true."

He nods.

"You know what? I believe you. I been checking up on you. I had guys watching you at that store you work at. I could see you were playing straight. And so I never came after you. Because I knew you weren't coming after me. I could see you just wanted to let things lie."

Juan, Chucho and Snap are listening to this with their mouths hanging open. Even the baby has stopped crying. I'm glad, because she makes me think of Emilio.

"But now this happened," says Lencho. He kicks Martín in the side. Martín whimpers.

"And so you know what? I'm making a pronouncement. This little punk is no longer a Vandal. He's out. He's fair game. And I don't care what happens to him."

"Lencho, please," says Martín.

"Shut up," says Lencho. "Martín, you got a two-minute head start. Get up and run, punk. Run to save yourself. 'Cause ain't nobody else gonna save you."

Martín gets to his feet. He looks around, his eyes wild. Then he turns and runs out of the room.

"You catch him, he's yours," Lencho says to Juan.

Juan nods. I can see he and the other two guys are itching to go after him. They're not going to wait two minutes. Two seconds, maybe. Martín doesn't stand a chance.

"Loco," says Lencho.

We look into each other's eyes.

"I'm sorry about your brother," he says.

I nod.

"So am I," I say.

"So let this be the end of it."

"That's right."

"I hope your lady is gonna be okay."

I don't say anything to that, because I don't know if she is or not.

But I do know one thing.

It's over.

Juan looks at Chucho and Snap. They nod. Then Juan looks at me. I don't say anything. I just shake my head. I'm not going to be a part of this. I'm done.

"You guys go," says Juan. "I'm gonna take Loco back to the hospital."

Chucho and Snap roll out of the room.

And I'm very glad that I'm not Martín.

CHAPTER FIFTEEN

I open the door of the ICU as quiet as I can. It seems kind of silly, with the hospital being such a loud place. There's doctors being paged, babies crying, nurses yelling to each other down the hall, and people running around everywhere. But I can see through the window that Connie and Emilio are sleeping. I don't want to wake them up.

I pull up a chair and sit next to them. For a while I just watch. They look so peaceful. Emilio has a little blue hat on. I haven't even seen his eyes yet. He keeps them scrunched up tight. I bet the world must seem like a pretty bright place when you've never seen lights before.

After a while Connie's eyes open.

"Baby," I say, "I'm here."

I reach for her hand. But she pulls it away. Then she starts to cry.

"What's the matter?" I say.

"You lied to me," she says.

"What? No, I didn't lie about anything," I tell her. "What are you talking about?"

"What is that on your head?" she asks. "If you didn't lie, why are you wearing that?"

Oh, man. I was so excited to get back to the hospital, I forgot I was still wearing Tomás's bandana. I reach up and take it off my head.

"You don't understand," I say.

"What is there to understand? You're back in the gang."

"I just…I…" I search for the right words to explain. But they don't come. I can't lie to her. But would she understand the truth?

"There was something I had to settle," I tell her. "About who shot you. I had to make things right. So nothing like this would ever happen again. But I didn't hurt anybody. And I swear, I haven't broken my promise."

"I wish I could believe you," she whispers.

"Connie, listen. Have I ever lied to you before?"

She shakes her head.

"That's right. And I'm not lying now. From now on, there won't be any more trouble. I took care of everything. And I did it in a way you would be proud of. Please, Connie. You and Emilio are the most important things in my world."

"You swore to me," she said. "You said you would never wear the colors again."

"Yeah," I admit, "I did say that. And I'm sorry I broke that promise. But Connie, sometimes you have to break little promises so that you can keep the big ones."

"What does that mean?"

"It means…it means I'm here for you. Now and forever. I won't ever put this on again. I won't have to."

"Are the cops gonna come looking for you?"

"No. They have no reason to."

"You promise?"

"Yes, baby, I promise."

Emilio starts to wake up. First he fusses, making those little kitten noises. It's dim in the room. The only light comes from the machines that are helping Connie. And he opens his eyes for the first time. They're big and dark, like his mama's.

"Hey, he's awake," I say.

Connie looks down at him.

"I dreamed I was all alone with him," she says. "All alone in the world, without you to take care of us."

"That was a bad dream," I say. "And it won't come true."

Connie looks at me for a long time.

I look into her eyes, so she knows I'm serious. Emilio fusses again.

"Can I hold him?" I ask.

Connie nods. I stand and pick him up like he's made out of glass. He weighs almost nothing. The blankets are heavier than he is. I cradle him in my arm and look down at his face. Emilio looks up into my eyes.

I'm not ready for what I see there. He's innocent. Defenseless. And he trusts me. I can see that. Nobody ever looked at me like that before. Not even Connie. It almost breaks my heart. Was this how my dad looked at me, when I was born? I'll never know for sure. But I like to think we had a moment like this, even if it only lasted for a few seconds.

"He's perfect," I say.

Emilio starts to cry. But it's a good cry. Healthy. Strong.

"He's hungry," Connie says.

A nurse comes in and helps Connie sit up. Then Connie starts to feed him.

Emilio makes little grunting noises as he drinks his mama's milk. His face is pressed so far into her breast it disappears.

"He's got a good appetite," I say.

"He eats like his daddy," says Connie.

"Mr. Gomez, your wife still needs rest," says the nurse. "You'd better leave them alone for a while."

"I'll be outside," I tell Connie. "I'm not leaving this place again unless you come with me."

"Okay," says Connie. I can tell by the look on her face that she finally believes me.

I go out into the waiting room. Juan is there.

"Man, you're still here? What are you doing here?" I ask.

"Waiting, dude. What else would I be doing in a waiting room?"

"You don't have to wait. You can leave. Everything's cool."

"Good. Man, this place is driving me

crazy," he says. "No offense, homes, but I don't think I want to come back here anymore."

"No problem," I say. "Thanks for the ride."

I've got Tomás's bandana in my hand. I hold it out to Juan.

"I don't need this," I say.

"Not even to remember your brother?"

I shake my head.

"I got everything I need to remember him right here," I say, pointing to my heart.

Juan takes the bandana. Then he ties it around his wrist.

"I'll wear this for your brother," he says. "And for you. You did good today."

"It's all done now," I say.

Juan nods.

"I watched you through the window for a second," he says. "I could see how happy you were, holding your son. And you know something?"

"What?"

"I get it now," he says. "I'm sorry for the things I said to you before. Now I understand why you left. You're where you belong."

"Thanks," I say.

"But the Kings will never forget you for helping them."

"How did I help them?"

"You made peace," Juan says. "Nobody else could have done that but you. We were all set up for war. But people would have died. Innocent people. Maybe even someone's little baby. I didn't know Lencho had a kid. That could have been really bad. And it made me think."

"You know, Juan, it's not too late for you," I say. "It's never too late to change."

Juan looks at me. Then he smiles. It's not a big smile. I don't think Juan can ever really be happy. Not after all he's seen and done. But I've never seen him smile before. Something has changed inside him.

We don't say anything more. He reaches out to give me the handshake. But he changes his mind, and instead we hug.

Then Juan turns and walks out of the waiting room. Just like that, he's gone.

I sit down and close my eyes. I'm bone tired, more tired than I've ever been. I need to call Mr. Enwright and explain things to him. I hope I still have a job.

And I need to call Tia Carlita and let her know the baby is here.

But first, I need to sleep.

Just before I nod off, I wonder if I'll ever see Juan again. Maybe, maybe not. But I like to think I got through to him a little bit. I hope he thinks about me and my family. I hope he remembers how he felt when he was looking in at us through the window.

And I hope that the next time he has to make a hard choice, thinking about us helps him do the right thing...whatever that may be.

CHAPTER SIXTEEN

Graduation Day. I've never seen so many people in one place. There are a few hundred of us students sitting in hard folding chairs. We're in the middle of a big auditorium. But in the stands, there are thousands of people. Everyone's family is here. I know they all came out to cheer for their loved ones. But I feel like everyone is looking right at me. My face is getting hot.

I look down at my shoes. They're as shiny as a mirror. Connie polished them for me. I told her I would do it, but she wouldn't let me. She said she wished she had enough money to buy me a present, but this was the best she could do. I told her I didn't need a present. Just having her home was enough.

She's out there somewhere, along with Emilio and Tia Carlita. Carlita brought all her kids. So did everyone else. The place is a madhouse. The president of the community college has to shout into the microphone. Even then, I can barely hear him. But maybe that's just because I'm so nervous. More nervous than I was in the car on the way to Lencho's house. More nervous than when I called Mr. Enwright to tell him I was sorry for leaving work. More nervous than I've ever been in my life. Because my dream is about to come true.

I stick my head up and look around. I'm trying to find Connie. But she's lost in the sea of faces. This must be what it feels like to be a rock star. No, thanks. Not for me. I'll take my job at the supermarket any day. I don't like this much attention.

The president gives a speech. Then the dean gives one. Then some other dude I never heard of. The speeches go on and on. The air is getting hot. I'm thirsty, and I'm starting to fall asleep. Emilio was up fussing last night. He's a good baby, but babies cry. Connie still has trouble getting out of bed, so I'm the one who gets him from the crib. Then I bring him into our bed so Connie can nurse him. I didn't even want her to come today. She's still sore from her surgery. But she said she would make it even if it killed her. I worked too long for this for her to stay home. I told her, "Baby, we both worked for it. And we both deserve this day. It's been a long road."

Finally, they start calling names.

They get through the As and Bs and into the Cs and Ds. My palms are starting to sweat. E and F take forever. Then he starts in on the Gs.

I can't believe it. I can't believe I'm here. It's finally happening. I'm about to graduate from high school.

Garfield, Arthur.

Ginsberg, Michelle.

Gomez, Rosario.

Hey, wait a minute. That's me.

I get up and pray my knees don't give out on me. I walk past all the other people in my row. Then I head up the stairs to the platform. It's full of people in black robes and funny square hats. I'm wearing a funny square hat too. It feels weird on my head, like it's about to fall off. I keep wanting to grab it to make sure it doesn't. But I keep my hands at my sides. Back straight. Look straight ahead.

I cross the platform. The president is an old man with gold glasses. It seems like he's a million miles away. But suddenly I'm standing in front of him. He's holding out a piece of paper, all rolled up.

I take it.

The president shakes my hand.

"Congratulations, Mr. Gomez," he says.

I don't even remember if I said anything or not. All I know is I feel like I'm floating a foot above the platform. I float across it and go down the stairs. Then I float back to my seat. I sit down, shaking. I look around again.

Then I see her. She's standing up, waving. Emilio is in her arms.

Maybe it's bad manners. But I can't help it. I stand up, too, and wave my diploma in the air.

I mouth the words, "I love you."

She mouths the same thing back.

I'm a high-school graduate.

*   *   *

Later, when it's all over, I make my way through the people to find Connie. She gives me a big hug. Carlita and her kids are all talking at once. I put my arm around Connie, and we start to leave the auditorium. There's a big party happening somewhere, and everyone is invited. But it's time to feed Emilio, and Connie needs a nap. I don't even care. I don't need a party. I got everything I need, right here.

We step out of the building and onto the sidewalk. It's a beautiful day. The sky is blue, the air is warm. Everyone is in a good mood.

"Hey, look at that," says Connie.

She points. I look to see what it is. Next to the street is a big old tree. And the branches look like they're alive. Thousands of little things are fluttering in it.

"What are those?" says Connie.

I squint. I can't believe my eyes. But I should have known something like this would happen. Your real family never leaves you, even when you think they're gone.

"They're butterflies," I say. "There must be a million of them."

"I've never seen so many before," says Connie.

"Me neither," I say.

"They're beautiful."

"The most beautiful thing I've ever seen," I say.

We head down the sidewalk to the bus stop. I want to take off my cap and gown, but Connie makes me leave them on. "Okay," I say. "Just for fun." She wants everyone to know what I did today. She's so proud, it's almost funny.

We get on the bus and sit down. It pulls out, and we start the long journey home.

Tomorrow I have to get up earlier than normal. It's my first day at my new job. I'm still at the supermarket. But now I've got a new title. I am Rosario Gomez, Assistant Manager. To celebrate, I bought myself a new shirt and pair of pants. I got a new tie too.

And starting tomorrow, something else is going to be different. I'm not going to

keep my right hand in my pocket anymore.
I don't have to advertise my tattoo, but I
don't have to be ashamed of it either. I'm
not a King anymore. But they're a part of
who I was. And who I was is a part of who
I am. I'm not ashamed of myself anymore.
I've just got my eye on the future, instead
of the past.

I know I have a long way to go. But the
important thing is, I'm on the way. I can see
myself in a three-piece suit, flying around
the country, or maybe even the world.
I'm shaking hands, making deals. Doing
business.

And I know that as long as I can see it,
it's going to happen.

My name is Rosario Gomez.

And I'm going to be a success.

WILLIAM KOWALSKI is the bestselling, award-winning author of many novels, including seven books in the Rapid Reads line. His first novel, *Eddie's Bastard*, won the 1999 Rosenstein Award, the 2001 Ama-Boeke Prize, and occupied the #5 spot on the Times of London bestseller list. His fifth novel, *The Hundred Hearts*, won the 2014 Thomas H. Raddall Atlantic Fiction Award. He has been nominated three times for the Ontario Library Association's Golden Oak Award and his books have been translated into fifteen languages. William lives with his family in Nova Scotia.